This book belongs to

_____

THE EMPEROR'S NEW CLOTHES

Illustrated by
Michael Adams

Story by

HANS CHRISTIAN ANDERSEN

The Unicorn Publishing House
New Jersey

any years ago there was an Emperor who was so very fond of new clothes that he spent all his money on them. He cared nothing about his soldiers, nor for the theater, nor for riding in the woods except for the sake of showing off his new clothes. He had a costume for every hour in the day. Instead of saying as one does about any other king or emperor, "He is in his council chamber," the people here always said, "The Emperor is in his dressing room."

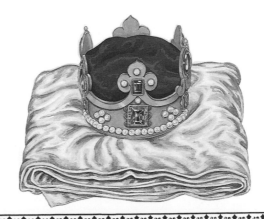

Life was very gay in the great town where he lived. Hosts of strangers came to visit it every day, and among them one day were two swindlers. They told everyone that they were weavers and said that they knew how to weave the most beautiful fabrics imaginable. Not only were the colors and patterns very fine, but the clothes that were made of this cloth had the peculiar quality of becoming invisible to every person who was not fit for the office he held, or who was impossibly dull.

"Those must be splendid clothes," thought the Emperor. "By wearing them I should be able to discover which men in my kingdom are not fit for their posts. I shall distinguish the wise men from the fools. Yes, I certainly must order some of that stuff to be woven for me."

The Emperor paid the two swindlers a lot of money in advance, so that they might begin their work at once.

They did put up two looms and pretended to weave, but they had nothing whatever upon their shuttles. They asked for a quantity of the finest silk and the purest gold thread, all of which they put into their own bags while they worked away at the empty looms far into the night.

"I should like to know how those weavers are getting on with their cloth," thought the Emperor, but he felt a little queer when he reflected that anyone who was stupid or unfit for his post would not be able to see it. He certainly thought that he need have no fears for himself, but still he thought he would send somebody else first to see how it was getting on. Everybody in the town knew what wonderful power the stuff possessed, and everyone was anxious to see how stupid his neighbor was.

"I will send my faithful old minister to the weavers," thought the Emperor. "He will be best able to see how the stuff looks, for he is a clever man and no one fulfills his duties better than he does."

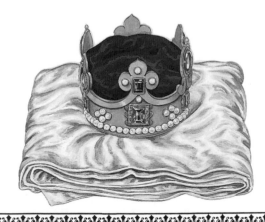

So the good old minister went into the room where the two swindlers sat working at the empty loom.

"Heaven help us," thought the old minister, opening his eyes very wide. "Why, I can't see a thing!" But he took care not to say so.

Both the swindlers begged him to be good enough to step a little nearer, and asked if he did not think it a good pattern and beautiful coloring. They pointed to the empty loom. The poor old minister stared as hard as he could, but he could not see anything, for of course there was nothing to see.

"Good heavens," thought he. "Is it possible that I am a fool? I have never thought so, and nobody must know it. Am I not fit for my post? It will never do to say that I cannot see the stuff."

"Well, sir, you don't say anything about the stuff," said the one who was pretending to weave.

"Oh, it is beautiful—quite charming," said the minister, looking through his spectacles. "Such a pattern and such colors! I will certainly tell the Emperor that the stuff pleases me very much."

"We are delighted to hear you say so," said the swindlers, and then they named all the colors and described the peculiar pattern. The old minister paid great attention to what they said, so as to be able to repeat it when he got home to the Emperor.

Then the swindlers went on to demand more money, more silk, and more gold, so they could go on with the weaving. But they put it all into their own pockets. Not a single strand was ever put into the loom, but they went on as before, weaving at the empty loom.

The Emperor soon sent another faithful official to see how the stuff was getting on and if it would soon be ready. The same thing happened to him as to the minister. He looked and looked, but as there was only the empty loom, he could see nothing at all.

"Is not this a beautiful piece of stuff?" said both the swindlers, showing and explaining the beautiful pattern and colors which were not there to be seen.

"I know I am no fool," thought the man, "so it must be that I am unfit for my good post. It is very strange, though. However, one must not let it appear." So he praised the stuff he did not see, and assured them of his delight in the beautiful colors and the originality of the design.

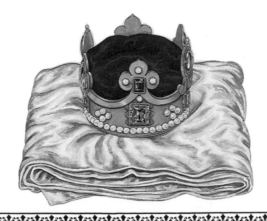

"It is absolutely charming," he said to the Emperor. Everybody in the town was talking about this splendid stuff.

Now the Emperor thought he would like to see it while it was still on the loom. So, accompanied by a number of selected courtiers, among whom were the two faithful officials who had already seen the imaginary stuff, he went to visit the crafty impostors, who were working away as hard as ever they could at the empty loom.

"It is magnificent," said both the honest officials. "Only see, Your Majesty, what a design! What colors!" And they pointed to the empty loom, for they each thought no doubt the others could see the stuff.

"What?" thought the Emperor. "I see nothing at all. This is terrible! Am I a fool? Am I not fit to be Emperor? Why, nothing worse could happen to me!"

"Oh, it is beautiful," said the Emperor. "It has my highest approval." And he nodded his satisfaction as he gazed at the empty loom. Nothing would induce him to say that he could not see anything.

The whole group gazed and gazed, but saw nothing more than all the others. However, they all exclaimed with His Majesty, "It is very beautiful." And they advised him to wear a suit made of this wonderful cloth on the occasion of a great procession which was just about to take place.

"Magnificent! Gorgeous! Excellent!" went from mouth to mouth. They were all equally delighted with it. The Emperor gave each of the rogues an order of knighthood to be worn in their buttonholes and the title of "Gentleman Weaver."

The swindlers sat up the whole night before the day on which the procession was to take place, burning sixteen candles, so that people might see how anxious they were to get the Emperor's new clothes ready. They pretended to take the stuff off the loom. They cut it out in the air with a huge pair of scissors, and they stitched away with needles without any thread in them.

At last they said, "Now the Emperor's new clothes are ready."

The Emperor with his grandest courtiers went to them himself, and both swindlers raised one arm in the air, as if they were holding something. They said, "See, these are the trousers. This is the coat. Here is the mantle," and so on. "It is as light as a spider's web. One might think one had nothing on, but that is the very beauty of it."

"Yes," said all the courtiers, but they could not see anything, for there was nothing to see.

"Will Your Imperial Majesty be graciously pleased to take off your clothes?" said the impostors. "Then we may put on the new ones, along here before the great mirror."

The Emperor took off all his clothes, and the impostors pretended to give him one article of dress after the other of the new ones which they had pretended to make. They pretended to fasten something around his waist and to tie on something. This was the train, and the Emperor turned round and round in front of the mirror.

"How well His Majesty looks in the new clothes! How becoming they are!" cried all the people round. "What a design, and what colors! They are most gorgeous robes."

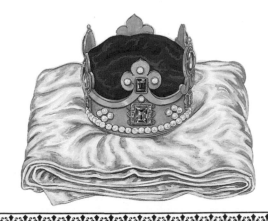

"The canopy is waiting outside which is to be carried over Your Majesty in the procession," said the master of the ceremonies.

"Well, I am quite ready," said the Emperor. "Don't the clothes fit well?" Then he turned round again in front of the mirror, so that he should seem to be looking at his grand things.

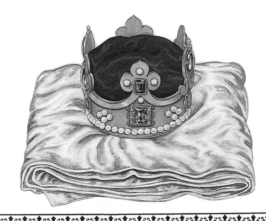

The chamberlains who were to carry the train stooped and pretended to lift it from the ground with both hands, and they walked along with their hands in the air. They dared not let it appear that they could not see anything.

Then the Emperor walked along in the procession under the gorgeous canopy, and everybody in the streets and at the windows exclaimed, "How beautiful the Emperor's new clothes are! What a splendid train! And they fit to perfection!"

Nobody would let it appear that he could see nothing, for then he would not be fit for his post, or else he was a fool. None of the Emperor's clothes had been so successful before.

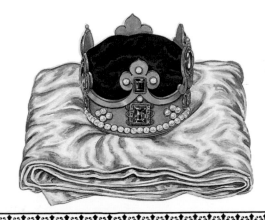

"But he has got nothing on," said a little child.

"Oh, listen to the innocent," said the father. And one person whispered to the other what the child had said. "He has nothing on—a child says he has nothing on!"

"But he has nothing on!" at last cried all the people.

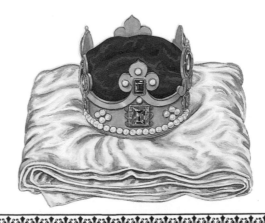

The Emperor writhed, for he knew it was true. But he thought, "The procession must go on now." So he held himself stiffer than ever, and the chamberlains held up the invisible train.

I would like to thank my family and friends who saw my vision — or did they? — while posing for me in this special edition of The Emperor's New Clothes:

CAST OF CHARACTERS

David Mainhart — The Emperor
Jim Stevens — The Thin Weaver
Harry N. Corpulent — The Fat Weaver
Jerry Ferlick — The Trusted Official, Townperson
Bob Adams — Minister
Laura Adams — Townsperson
Cathy Adams — Townsperson
Jude Adams — Townsperson
Ian Adams — Townsperson
Nick Adams — Townsperson
Michael Adams — Townsperson

Editor: John Ingram
Art Director: Heidi K.L. Corso
Printed in Singapore by Topan Printing Co., PTE. through Palace Press, San Francisco, CA
Cover and interior graphics © 1989 The Unicorn Publishing House. All Rights Reserved
Artwork © 1989 Michael Adams. All Rights Reserved
No copyrighted elements of this book may be reproduced in whole or in part, without written permission. For information, contact
The Unicorn Publishing House at 120 American Road, Morris Plains, NJ 07950.
Distributed to the book trade in Canada by Doubleday Canada, Ltd., Toronto, ON
Distributed to the toy and gift trade in Canada by Brigitta's Imports, Concord, ON

Printing History 15 14 13 12 11 10 9 8 7 6 5 4 3 2 1

Library of Congress Cataloging-in-Publication-Data

Andersen, H.C. (Hans Christian), 1805-1875.
[Kejserens nye klaeder. English]
The emperor's new clothes / by Hans Christian Andersen; illustrated by Michael Adams. p. cm.
Summary: Two rascally weavers convince the emperor they are making him beautiful new clothes, visible only to those fit for their posts, but during a royal procession in which he first wears them, a child whispers that the emperor has nothing on.
ISBN 0-88101-095-2
[1. Fairy Tales.] I. Adams, Michael, ill. II Title.
PZ8.A542Em 1989
[E]—dc 19 89-4804
CIP   AC

Other Delightful Stories
Richly Illustrated in Unicorn's
Through the Magic Window Series:

WYNKEN, BLYNKEN, AND NOD
PETER COTTONTAIL'S SURPRISE